FETCH THE FLAME

KAY'S INTERLUDE

A Dance of the Elements Story

A.M. DEESE

This is a work of fiction. All characters and events portrayed in this novel are either products of the author's imagination or are used fictitiously.

FETCH THE FLAME

Cover by DRIVEN Digital Services at drivends.com
Editing and typesetting by Kingsman Editing at kingsmanediting.com

First Edition July 2019
ISBN: 9780999160817

www.amdeese.com

This book is dedicated to everyone who has read *Ignited*
and for those who begged for more Kay.

Author's Note

Although *Fetch the Flame* is a complete story, the novelette is part of a much larger story arc found in the Dance of the Elements series. This story takes place between books one and two in the series and follows a fan favorite, Kay, a precocious and powerful seven-year-old girl. For more information on the series and for book one, *Ignited*, please check out my website at www.amdeese.com.

CONTENTS

ONE

A New Day and New Name

For the first time since she'd been taken, Kay opened her eyes and knew exactly where she was. The early morning light forced her to squint; someone had positioned the beds in just the right spot so that dawn woke her with its blinding radiance no matter what bed she chose to sleep in. She frowned down at the row of empty beds and reached blindly for the small glass of water on her bedside table.

Every morning there was a fresh glass of water. She wondered who had the job of sneaking in her room at night and placing it there. Ash perhaps? He seemed to be in charge of her now. She drank the morning's rations and thought of the crisp water from the well back on her family's property. Somehow the water was always cold, even in the middle of the summer. Here in the Sand Sea, the summer never ended.

So far no one had yelled at her about the big fire wall she'd brought on Timber. Maybe everyone knew that he had deserved it, that he shouldn't have been sparring so roughly. Kay didn't even feel bad, not exactly. She would do it again if it meant saving Kindle. She was so nice. Kindle had explained that Kay wasn't in trouble, but she had tucked her into her tiny house—*barracks*, she remembered the word with a soft smile—before the sun had even gone down. But that was yesterday. Surely she wouldn't be punished today for something that happened yesterday. She was frowning over this idea when the heavy door scraped against the dirty floor.

"Good morning, Cadet."

Kay frowned at the new name. It had started last night, after her display of firepower. Maybe she had done a bad thing after all. She didn't want a new name.

Kindle gave her a warm smile and repeated the words in Jangba. The language of the Sand Sea sounded garbled and strange, an odd mash-up of lyrical rolls and harsh vowels. Kay repeated the words in her head though she didn't bother saying them out loud. She couldn't easily twist her tongue from one language to the next as Kindle did.

"I know you want to go home," Kindle continued in Drakori, repeating herself in Jangba, "but home is a long ways away and now that you've proven how talented you are, it's time for you to truly begin your training." She paused. Her eyes looked so worried, so *nice*. Kindle was pretty in the way a dragon was beautiful. She had a fearsome scar over one eye that disappeared whenever she smiled. It reminded her of Mama's dimples.

"My training?" Kay asked and quickly repeated the word in Jangba at Kindle's frown.

"Yes, you're a cadet now, training to be a Fire Dancer like myself, like Ash." Kindle raised her eyebrows. "Ash waits for you in the sands. And you're late."

Kay blinked, struggling to process the translations. How was she late for something she didn't even know about? And training! Did that mean she would be like one of the boys she'd seen dancing with sticks? Was this really what this had all been about?

"Hustle, Cadet."

That phrase, "Hustle, Cadet," was repeated enough times throughout the morning that Kay was sure she could repeat it without a trace of an accent. Ash snapped directions at her in rapid succession. Kindle stood at his shoulder, shouting out random interpretations because surely Ash was screaming out more than "Point your toe."

She almost fell to the sand in relief when Kindle translated it was time for a water break.

Kay gulped down the ration greedily, searching for more.

"That's all, Cadet. You get more in your afternoon ration."

What? That didn't make sense. She was *dying* of thirst. "I'm thirsty now!" she whined in Drakori, stomping her foot for good measure. Mama would have been horrified but she didn't care.

Apparently, neither did Kindle because she stood and said some quiet words to Ash. The two spoke for a moment as Kay watched them, silently fuming. Finally, Kindle turned back to Kay. She had a new smile on her face, this one somewhat sad.

"I have to go to my own training session, so I have to leave you now. You have fire motion training next. I think you'll like it." Kindle reached over and pushed the curls back from Kay's face. "I'm sorry I can't stay."

And just as quickly, she left.

Ash took hold of Kay's empty water skin and gestured for her to follow him to the next field. This arena was larger than the others and was surrounded by a ring of torches. What was the point of so many when it was barely the afternoon?

She followed Ash into the ring, but they stayed on the

perimeter as the center was already occupied by Timber—the big guy who'd challenged Kindle—and a boy a few years older than herself. The boy was also special. Maybe, everyone here was. A tiny idea began to form. She latched onto it as she watched the boy pull the fire from the two torches on either side of him. He held the tiny sputtering flames just above either hand, smiling in triumph. Kay rolled her eyes. Piece of cake. He wasn't even using his own flame. He was basically cheating. Moving a dead flame like that took about as much effort as holding a bubble of soap.

She realized Ash was speaking to her so she squinted in concentration and really did try to understand what he was saying. Something about looking or watching, and something about holding hands with the fire. That couldn't be right. She nodded blandly and he mimicked the nod with a friendly grin.

The boy in the center of the ring was now juggling the two flames, sending each higher and higher into the sky.

"What's his name?" Kay asked in Jangba, surprising even herself.

"He is Cadet," Ash answered.

Kay rolled her eyes again and received a frown from Ash.

"His name. My name Kay, his name— "

"His name is Cadet."

Kay frowned. Well that couldn't be right. Did Ash mean that his name was also Kay? That somehow Kay in this language translated into Cadet? But no . . . That boy across the field, he was also called Cadet. The word had to mean someone who was still young and in training because all the adults had their own name. So what did it all mean? What was she training for? A Fire Dancer, Kindle had said. But what was the purpose of all of it?

Looking around, Kay realized the field was full of the so-called Fire Dancers. The adults fought each other two at a time, thrusting their tall sticks and twirling around one another. She noted another woman aside from Kindle, but she didn't notice any girls near her own age.

Ash tapped her shoulder, bringing her attention back to the center ring where the cadet had added a third fireball to his juggling act. Kay sighed. What was so important about watching this boy juggle? She nodded along to Ash's stream of words and waited for the boy to finish. He had begun to draw a crowd. The big man with him tossed the boy yet another fireball. He caught it awkwardly, and for a moment, Kay thought he would drop the flame, but within seconds he'd gained control and forced it in rotation with the others. His triumphant grin would have made Kay roll her eyes again, but a hand brushed against hers, distracting her.

"Don't look over. Don't let anyone notice you're talking to me."

Kay couldn't help her gaze sliding over at the sound of a familiar language and unexpected touch. She stared down at her hands once she recognized the face. It was Wallace, the boy who had taken the beating for talking to her, back when they had still been under Udo's care. If she could call it care. Udo was the man responsible for transporting her from her home here to the Sand Sea. He was a terrible man, and seeing Wallace again made her skin prickle.

"What are you doing here? Are you special too?"

"Special." The boy grunted. "You could say that."

"Did you get taken from your home too?" She dared a quick glance at Ash, but his attention remained on the struggling fire juggler and not on the young girl talking to her feet beside him.

"You're younger than I thought you were."

Kay bristled at his observation. Like he was an adult. What did it matter how old she was anyway?

"Don't get mad." His fingers bumped into hers. "It was just

an observation. I've been looking for you."

Why? She voiced the thought out loud and dared another quick glance at the boy's face. He was probably around ten or eleven. His skin was bruised, and his hair hung in disheveled layers that framed his wide face as if someone had chopped it with a knife. He was taller than she remembered.

"Because you're like me. Because you don't deserve to be here. Because I'm escaping and heading back home where I belong. And I'm taking you with me."

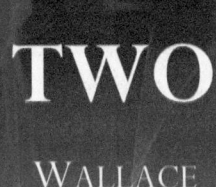

TWO

WALLACE

Freedom, home. He promised everything her heart desired. The boy's hand bumped into hers yet again, and this time Kay felt a tiny scrap of paper clenched between his fingers. She took it from him, slipping it into her pocket just as Ash placed a heavy palm on her shoulder.

Ash mumbled a string of words, none of which Kay understood so she remained still until a gentle shove from Ash had her walking to the center of the ring.

It was blazing hot. Surrounded by the flickering torches and under the harsh sun and scorching sands, Kay felt she could ignite the entire field with a mere flick of her little finger. But surely that wasn't Ash's intention. She waited silently, struggling not to fidget. The note from Wallace, if it was indeed a note, seemed to burn a hole in her pocket.

Ash called out to her, gesturing to the torches. She wasn't entirely sure what he expected of her. Did he want her to simply juggle fireballs like the boy before her? It seemed as good as any guess. She looked at the torches and kept her breathing normal, focusing instead on the motion of the dead flames. There would have been ten of them had the boy bothered to put the flames back after he'd juggled them. But he had allowed one to sputter out and the others had fallen to the sand forgotten.

Kay was *really* good at juggling flames. She'd tried juggling real balls just earlier that summer and that had been a disaster. Actual balls had to follow the rules of gravity, and Kay had been unable to get all three balls in the air at one time. Daddy had laughed so hard.

She blinked a few times in rapid succession to make sure she didn't cry. It had been a mistake to think of Daddy. It was Wallace's fault for making her think of home. The boy was gone, the spot next to Ash empty, and the retired Fire Dancer gave her an encouraging smile. She took a deep Breath and one torch sputtered out.

Compared to actual balls, juggling fire was easy, especially fire that was alive and her own. She Breathed in the remaining four torches and shot out ten streams of fire from each of her fingertips. Then ten tiny fireballs spun around her head and into the air, circling the length of her body.

She grinned at the watching cadet. His mouth hung slightly open.

Kay began to juggle the ten fireballs, at times tossing one or more behind her back to juggle sideways. Yeah, juggling fire was way easier than balls. She spun the fireballs around a few more times for good measure before sending the individual flames to reignite each of the torches.

Afterward there was more than one gaping face. Strangely, Ash appeared more angry than amazed. She met eyes with the cadet who had juggled before her and he scowled. Her smile faltered.

Ash snapped out orders she didn't understand followed by

the familiar command, "Hustle, Cadet." She hurried off the field toward him and he directed her to the fence line, making a wide sweeping motion with his hand. She frowned, unsure what he wanted. He repeated his command and pointed again to the fence line.

"Go on, laps for conditioning. Start running. Hustle, Cadet."

She ran to the fence line, but when she began to run back, Ash made another circular motion with his hand. Finally understanding his command, she began to run in large circles around the field. The other cadets joined her, and within minutes, there were nearly a dozen of them packed tightly around her as they made their laps.

Wallace shouldered his way beside her, breathing hard. He towered over her. He had to be at least four or five years older than her own seven years, but then, it seemed everyone here was a bit older than she was.

"You can read, right?"

"Of course I can read!" she exclaimed indignantly. She'd been reading as long as she could remember.

"Shh, quiet. Don't let them see us talking. These people . . ." He trailed off, his expression haunted.

Kay didn't know how to respond. Ash hadn't harmed her . . . yet. She remembered Udo's heavy boot and shuddered even though she ran in the searing heat.

"Do you really think you can get us back home?" All the hope in the world hung on that one sentence.

"We'll talk tonight. Just be careful in the meantime. And don't trust anyone here, no matter how nice they seem." He pulled ahead and she didn't bother to keep pace, not when she was already gasping for breath.

THREE

The *completion of the laps* brought with it the sweet afternoon ration of water. Kay gulped hers down in a hurry. It was better not to taste the warm coppery stuff anyway. Her fingers itched to brush against the tiny scrap of paper in her pocket, but she knew better than to reach for it again. She couldn't call any attention to it, especially not before she saw what it said for herself.

Kindle returned, sweaty and bruised. She gave Kay a quick grin before she and Ash spoke in quiet tones. Kay finished her water and strained to hear anything that was said, but the adults spoke in Jangba and Kay could barely hear as it was. After a few moments, when Kay was good and bored, Kindle turned her attention to her.

"I hear you had a good showing at fire motion class."

That had been a class? Kay frowned. She certainly hadn't learned anything, not if she didn't count the note in her pocket.

"I like juggling with fire," Kay mumbled.

"Why didn't you tell me before? When you first arrived?

Were you frightened?"

Even though they were said in her native tongue, the barrage of questions was overwhelming. She nodded in response and Kindle sighed.

"I'm sorry. Of course you were frightened. Especially after . . . well whatever it is you went through." Kindle's voice was now soft and soothing, the voice Mama reserved for bedtime stories.

It was a voice Kay would never hear again. She suddenly hated Kindle and her voice that was so like Mama's but would never be Mama.

"I want to go to my room."

Kindle shook her head. "Not just yet little one. First you have a tutoring session. We need to get you speaking Jangba."

"I can't," Kay said in perfect Jangba, because this was one phrase she had learned.

Kindle sighed but she remained patient, her arms folded over her chest, and she simply stood waiting for Kay to follow her to her studies. Apparently she would have to do work before she was free to read Wallace's note.

"Okay, I'll study."

Kindle didn't even scold her for her Drakori. She beckoned for Kay to follow her off the fields and, instead of heading back to her own barracks or Ash's room, Kindle directed her into the massive stone hallways that led to the great unknown.

"These are the arena halls." Kindle almost whispered the Drakori. She repeated herself in Jangba, a bit louder. "You must never attend these halls without proper escort, never without me or Ash."

Kay nodded, making the promise and pinching herself three times. If she had no intention of keeping a promise, three pinches were the standard punishment. Kindle didn't notice. She was too busy describing the difference between the stone hallways here and the sand walls of the barracks. Boring stuff.

The stone floors were swept and polished even though everyone crossing them had to be tracking sand. The walls were lined with torches and nothing else—no pictures or windows. It gave the hallway an ominous feel. To stop her shudder, Kay Breathed in the nearest torch.

She instantly felt more alive. As if she had Breathed in ten torches at once. Her skin burned, itched, *glowed* as the heat spread over her. It was both frightening and intoxicating.

She released the flame back to its place in the torch on the wall. It returned, sputtering wildly.

"The fire," she gasped loudly, drawing Kindle's attention.

"What is it? What's happening?" Kindle dropped into a fighter's stance Kay recognized from the practice fields.

Kay took another deep breath, feeling silly for her overreaction. "The fire." She pointed to the torch in question. "It felt different."

Kindle's shoulders relaxed. "That's something else I wanted to talk to you about. How you . . . eat the fire."

"I Breathe it," Kay answered automatically.

"Yes, you Breathe it in. Then what happens?" Kindle had stopped walking and had given Kay her full attention. It was scary. Adults very rarely gave her their full attention, well except for maybe Mama or Daddy. Kay shook her head.

"I Breathe it in and I feel strong and warm and then . . ." She shrugged. And then flames left her fingertips at her command, but she had been doing it for so long she didn't know how to explain it. How did one explain how their brain knew to raise the arm? It simply did. She pulled a flame from the wall, rolling it along the fingertips of her right hand. The flame still felt so different, almost like it was alive. But who had Breathed it and left it there?

The figures in red robes turned down their hall and Kindle quickly held a finger up to her lips, indicating that Kay should keep quiet. Kay replaced the flame on the torch and ducked closer to the Fire Dancer. They watched the group's approach with interest.

There were three of them, all in matching red cloaks that rippled behind them as they walked. Kay liked the color yet the air seemed to sizzle around them, and none of the three smiled.

Kindle bowed her head at their approach so Kay mimicked the action.

"Kindle Fire Dancer, well met."

"Well met," Kindle mumbled a quick reply without the smile she normally reserved for greetings.

Kay felt the man's eyes on her, but she only understood a few words, something about halls and cadets. She dared a quick glance at the speaker and was surprised to see he was an elderly man. The voice was deep and authoritative, its baritone echoing down the hall.

"This is the cadet of Ash Fire Dancer. I'm currently employed as a translator." Kindle repeated herself in Drakori.

The man scowled at Kindle's Drakori, and Kay found herself reaching for Kindle's hand. Whoever this man was, she'd decided she didn't like him.

"Ah, his wonder child." The old man turned and whispered to his companion in the matching robes. Kay stared at the tip of her ugly boots and tried to ignore the exchange of hushed tones. When he spoke again he said good-bye to them. Kay could understand the dismissive tone if not the actual words.

Kindle didn't have to tug her hand at all to get her to turn around and head back down the hall.

FOUR

THE MAP

Kay wanted to ask Kindle what all that had been about, but more than that, she wanted to read Wallace's letter. So she lied to Kindle and said she had a headache and wanted to go to sleep, and it seemed to work. The Fire Dancer escorted her back to her room and left her there, studies forgotten.

Kay had made a good show of it, whining over the heat then complaining about the coolness of her sheets once she was on her bed. Kindle had laid a warm hand over Kay's forehead, frowning as she'd done so but eventually she'd left. Kay lay in the bed another ten minutes or so before she was sure she wouldn't be disturbed and it was safe to open the note.

She pulled the rumpled parchment from where it was shoved deep in her pocket and smoothed it out on her lap. It wasn't a note but a map. The bottom of the page was an exact replica of the barracks with the surrounding halls and practice fields marked in precise clean strokes. Pathways were drawn from her room to another building across the fields, down the halls, and into the arena itself. *Wallace must be there*. She traced the path with her fingertip and landed on the building across from the fields. It was a wonderful map, beautifully drawn and seemingly accurate. But why had he given it to her? What was she supposed to do with this knowledge? There weren't any instructions.

Kay frowned, flipping the paper over to study the other side. *Meet me outside my barracks at midnight. Learn the map. Burn it. Tell no one.*

She flipped the map back over and studied it intently, memorizing the various pathways, especially those to the arena. Then she burned it all and waited for midnight.

She awoke with a wild gasp, clutching at the air. She wasn't supposed to fall asleep. That meant she'd lost track of all time. There were no clocks anywhere in her barracks. The only indication of the time came from a large gong that rang on the hour every hour. But if one fell asleep and missed count of the hours, there was no way to tell which one she was on. There was a chance she was early. There was also a chance she was very very late. Either way, she left her quiet building and slipped into the night. She was surprised to see the torches in the training fields had all been extinguished. She would have thought they would want the firelight now, but apparently no one was out venturing in the night. If they were, they stayed near the halls and their firepits. She followed the path Wallace had laid out in his map, circling wide around the training fields and creeping back up from behind his barracks. The building mirrored her own, except several voices were heard from inside. Wallace wasn't alone.

That was a good sign. She was probably early if everyone was still awake. Her belly growled and she considered walking over to the dining halls to see if dinner was still an option. But no, she couldn't risk running into Kindle or Ash. If they thought she was feeling better, she might have to study, never mind the questions she would have to answer. She recalled the flatbread left over from this morning's breakfast still sitting on her bedside table and was about to head back to her barracks when the door opened and a group of boys came out. There were four of them, all tall and much older than herself except for one. She recognized him as the boy who'd juggled fire before her in the ring today. She pressed herself closer to the door and hoped she was hidden in the shadows.

The boys didn't notice her though. They turned away from her and left toward the halls, laughing and shoving one another as they walked. Kay held her breath until they were well out of sight. It was quiet in the barracks, and once again Kay considered leaving for her room. The gong sounded in the distance, the sound vibrating the sand, and the door opened once again. It was Wallace.

FIVE

ANOTHER THREE PINCHES

Wallace *strolled out, leaning against* the wall of his building and studying his hands. His head turned toward her instantly when she stepped forward.

"You're just in time."

Kay smiled. "I'm surprised everyone is still awake. Where are all the boys going?"

Wallace shrugged but his face hardened, his mouth slashing downward. "Who cares about them. Did you burn the note like I told you to?"

She nodded.

"And you memorized the map?"

She nodded again.

"Good. Then we can begin phase one of the master plan."

"What's the master plan?" Kay scooted forward. Now that the bruises were fading, Kay could see that spattering of freckles across his nose and cheeks. Wallace frowned at her scrutiny.

"To break out of here, of course. To go back home. Don't you want to go back home?"

"I do, it's just . . ." Kay struggled to find the right words. "I don't have a home to go back to. My parents, the barn." She shook her head.

"I understand. Maybe you'll want to stay with me, at my home. I live with my big brother. He— " Wallace grabbed her shoulder and pushed her around to the side of the building, lowering his voice. "There are still some awake inside. We don't want to arouse suspicion." He gestured for her to follow him and set a brisk pace toward the arena halls where Kindle had taken her earlier. They stopped just outside the halls. Wallace pointed at them with a flick of his wrist.

"That's our way out."

The arena halls? Kay wrinkled her nose in concern. That didn't seem to make much sense. She stared at them now. A massive opening stretched into the great halls beyond. As far as Kay could tell, the walls were a corn maze made of stone with only the great arena at its center. She hadn't seen the arena yet, but even Daddy had told her stories about it. Back then, she'd never imagined she would someday see the dragon slayers in person—that she was maybe, possibly, training to be one. The thought sent another shiver down her spine. She'd been entertaining the idea for a while now, piecing together her experiences with the tales she'd heard of the great Republic of the Sand Sea.

"Not through the arena halls. Underneath them. I overhead my *owner* talking about them. There is a series of tunnels underneath the arena. It's how her dragon gets brought to the arena."

Kay thought of Ash, Kindle, and the fat man who often came to visit, the nice one who could also speak Drakori. He was probably her owner. At least Ash seemed to treat him as if that were so. Did he also bring his dragons in through these so-called catacombs? Because surely the man had dragons if he already owned several people. Kay made a mental note to ask Kindle about it tomorrow and struggled to remain focused on Wallace.

"We have to leave through the underground tunnels without anyone seeing us."

"Exactly. What we need to worry about is how to create a distraction big enough so no one is looking for two dumb kids sneaking underground."

Kay nodded, trying to look braver, older than she actually was. "I can do a distraction."

Wallace grinned and Kay realized he was missing the second tooth on his left side. She tried to smile back.

"I was hoping you would say that. You're special, you know that kid? All I need is one big display, just long enough to get into the arena halls and into those catacombs before anyone comes looking. We'll have to run straight to the market, but from there we can steal whatever we need to pay for passage home. Things will be easy. We just have to get outta here." There was an excited gleam to his eye, and his enthusiasm was infectious.

"I can do it." Kay whispered the words to herself, but Wallace heard her and agreed with her, thumping her soundly on the back with enough force to send her stumbling forward.

"There's just one thing kid. It's kinda important. You can't tell anyone about all this, okay? And I mean no one."

Kay nodded. She wouldn't want to tell Kindle or Ash anyway. They might try to stop her.

Wallace shook his head, his tone turning serious once again. "No, that's not enough. Swear it. Swear you won't tell anyone."

"I swear," Kay whispered back. His brown eyes stared deep into hers.

"Swear that you'll side with me above all others. Forsake all others here."

"I swear it," Kay said, louder.

Wallace grunted in approval and began to detail the rest of his master plan.

He didn't notice her pinch herself three times. She had to keep her options open, just in case.

SIX

LIARS AND THIEVES

T*he next morning brought with* it more blinding sunshine and another glass of stale water. Kay scowled at the cup but drank the water down in two gulps anyway. Water was water, whether it was yucky or not. She got dressed and made her way out to the training fields, meeting Kindle along the way.

"Good morning, Cadet." The Jangba rolled so easily off her tongue. Kay frowned but repeated the greeting in Jangba.

Kindle laughed in response. "We'll work on that accent. I have all day with you today. It's my off day and I'm going to spend it with you."

Kay bit her tongue and looked down at the ground. Stuck with Kindle babysitting her all day, she would never have an opportunity to sneak any conversations with Wallace. And today they were supposed to begin phase one of the master plan.

Kindle laughed again. "I'll try not to be hurt by your enthusiasm."

Kay knew what sarcasm was. Mama always said Daddy

was a sarcastic—Kay swallowed. It was so easy to remember her parents, so easy to forget they were gone.

Kindle placed a gentle hand on Kay's stiff shoulder.

"Hey, what's wrong?" She didn't even repeat herself in Jangba.

Kay shook her head. She didn't want to talk to Kindle about it. She couldn't open up to Kindle about one thing while lying about another. No, she had to focus on phase one of the master plan.

Phase one involved stealing.

Mama said people who lied and stole from others were the worst sort of people. If she knew of Kay's involvement in the plan, she would give her a good whipping. But it wasn't the first time she'd had to lie in these recent times, so what did it matter if she added stealing to the mix? It was unlikely Ash would need the dusty old map anyway. That's what Wallace had said.

Supposedly all retired Fire Dancers had them, the map of the catacombs. Wallace said that was part of what made Kay so perfect as his partner. They were meant to help each other. Kay took a deep breath and turned to Kindle with a smile. "I'm ready to go." She said the words in Jangba.

Moments later they arrived at the training field. The sun had just chased away the lingering soft pink hues, but it seemed everyone was already at practice. Despite her tardiness, Ash greeted her with a grin. He handed her a long stick, like the sort the boys carried. It had been freshly cut down to match her tiny size but despite this, the stick still towered over her.

"It's an assegai," Ash said. The reverent way he said the word made her study the stick more intently.

It was made of some sort of wood, smooth and warm beneath her fingers. The pole was straight save for the tip, which curved into a slight hook.

"I remember my first practice pole. Get comfortable with it. You'll need to take it with you everywhere. Get good enough with that thing and you'll get your glass tips in no time."

Kindle made short work of Ash's translation.

"Glass tips?" Kay asked.

Kindle nodded. "When you're ready for it, your training pole will be replaced by a proper weapon."

"I don't want to fight anyone," Kay whispered.

"You . . . We'll talk about it later. Ash is ready for you to take up first position. No, take your assegai with you."

Kay got her feet into their proper position, but she couldn't stop thinking about what it meant to hold a weapon. Only bad people needed weapons. But then again, maybe she was a bad person. She was a liar. She was planning on stealing from Ash. Her fingers tightened around the practice assegai. Maybe she needed a weapon after all.

SEVEN

PHASE ONE

There were *five different levels* or *Forms* as Ash called them. Each Form represented the color of a dragon. Orange, blue, black, green, and red. Red was the most difficult. Orange was a piece of cake once she got used to pointing her toes. Orange was truthfully nothing more than some weird foot positions and some easy spins.

It was important to Ash that she learn all the Forms. That much was obvious from his sharp tone and the frantic way he waved his arms. The Blue Form was more fun. It involved cartwheels and flips. Daddy was supposed to teach her to do a backflip this summer. Well, she would get to learn one anyway. It wasn't that hard. The key was to jump up really high before snapping her head back. Once she tucked up her knees, they seemed to fly naturally over her body. Kindle said Ash was barely spotting her at all and that she could probably do one by herself if she wanted.

Of course she wanted to. But before she could say anything she noticed the boy cadets had started running laps. It was the only time she was allowed any interaction with them, and the only opportunity she had to talk to Wallace before she went through with phase one.

"It's time to run laps." Kay pointed at the boys, making eye contact with Wallace as she did so.

"You don't have to run laps if you'd rather work on some more tumbling." Kindle smiled, but Kay shook her head so hard her curls bounced against her face. "No, I go run," she shouted.

Ash shrugged and said something like if she wants to run, let her run. Kindle gave her an odd look but took her assegai from her. Kay ran, panting hard as she elbowed her way through the crowd and up beside Wallace.

"Are you still ready for phase one?"

"I'm ready," Kay lied. She wasn't ready. But she would make sure she did her part. She wouldn't fail at this, not when it meant so much.

"It's not too late to back out."

"I said I'm ready!"

Wallace laughed. "Keep your voice down. Good. I'm glad you're ready. I am too. I'm going for my item tonight. You?"

"Tonight."

"Good. Meet afterward, same place, same time." He kept pace with her this time, but Kay had nothing left to say.

After a brief water break, it was time for another fire motion class, as Kindle called it. The trio approached the large ring, and Kay noticed this time only one of the torches was lit.

"Today's lesson you must light all the torches."

Kay blinked. Was that all? "I fire all the torches . . . and then class over?"

"Well done. She's learning Jangba so quickly," Ash exclaimed. He seemed proud.

"Fire motion class is completed, then you still have your

language studies." Kindle's voice had a slight edge of warning to it.

"Can I have language studies in Ash's room?" Though her studies had originated in his room, the last few days Kindle had taken to moving her around. First in the dining hall, then the library, and most recently, the arena halls. If she could get Kindle or Ash to show her the catacomb map, she would be halfway to completing her part of the plan.

"If Ash doesn't mind. Now no more talking. Pick up the flame and—Oh!" Kindle's scar disappeared beneath her widened eyes.

Kay hadn't meant to interrupt Kindle, but she said all she had to do was light the torches, and that was as easy as Breathing and pointing her fingers.

"Language studies in Ash room?"

Kindle blinked. "Let's go."

EIGHT

Ash's room wasn't far from the library. It was on the side of the halls where no one traveled. The side where everything was old and dusty. Ash wasn't old, even though his stubble was speckled with white. His dark, tanned skin was scratched and burned and pulled tight with muscle. No, he wasn't old. Ash probably wasn't much older than her daddy. He probably could have been his older brother. Daddy didn't have any siblings though and neither did Mama. They had both wanted them though, and Mama had promised Kay she would one day have siblings of her own. That would never happen now.

Kindle was kind of like a sister. She was nice and smart and bossy. Would Kay have been a bossy older sister? Kay pushed away thoughts of siblings and things she would never have and tried to concentrate. Daddy always said she had to visualize things. She thought of Ash's map to the catacombs and imagined herself holding it.

Ash wasn't in his room at the moment. Perhaps he was out

at dinner. He was seldom away from her, and Kay found herself wondering if Ash had any friends. Kindle was his friend at least, but he didn't seem to have any friends his own age, and none of the Fire Dancers seemed to have spouses. Kay asked Kindle about it, and the woman wrinkled her brow in confusion.

"No. Fire Dancers don't get married. It just doesn't make sense when we . . . do what we do." Kindle cleared her throat. "We should focus on your studies. Now, repeat the alphabet in Jangba."

"I can already do that," Kay whined, throwing herself onto Ash's bed. "Let's learn about something else. I want to learn about the arena!"

Kindle frowned. She seemed capable of ignoring Kay's big *please* expression. Mama was pretty good at ignoring it too.

Kindle let out a stream of words in rapid succession, and Kay shook her head. "What did you say?"

"I said," Kindle began and sent her a significant look, "I'm going to allow you to change the nature of your lesson if you agree to have the rest of the lesson in Jangba."

Kay groaned.

An hour later she was no closer to Ash's map, and Kindle hadn't even bothered bringing up the catacombs. At least Kay had found the map. It was beautiful really. The solid piece of glass had the twists and design of the catacombs etched into the glass by fire. They did that sometimes with maps they wanted to make sure stayed safe. It made sense, although it was odd that they made such fancy maps simply to hand them out to Fire Dancers who wouldn't need them.

Kindle noticed where she was staring and nodded toward the object. "Go on, bring it here."

Kay could barely contain her excitement as she walked over

to Ash's shelf and lifted the glass cube.

"It's so heavy," she gasped.

"Be careful," Kindle warned. "Ash made that himself. I imagine he'll be quite disappointed if he returns to find it broken."

"Careful, Cadet." The deep Jangba rang across the room, and Kay's head snapped up and her grip on the glass cube tightened.

"I was just telling her that," Kindle offered. She rose to her feet, greeting Ash with a smile.

"Sorry, in room." Kay stumbled over the words.

"It's fine," Ash said with a careless shrug. "Did you tell her about this thing?" Ash jerked his head in the direction of the glass cube that remained clutched between Kay's fingers.

"Everyone makes one. Eventually you will too," Kindle offered in Drakori. "Although not everyone's is as beautiful as Ash's. It's an honor and a keepsake to those retired from the arena. Once you are free enough to— "

"You're free?" Kay interrupted. She wanted to hear about the pretty glass map, but more important than that, she had to know if it was true.

"I earned my freedom just last season." Kindle's smile was proud. "Once you become a Fire Dancer, you can earn wages, and it's just a matter of time before you can purchase your freedom." She repeated herself in Jangba for Ash's benefit.

That would take years, and Kay didn't have years. She wanted to leave the arena as soon as possible, now if she could. No, earning her money as a Fire Dancer wouldn't work for her.

She wanted to know why they would choose to stay when either one could leave whenever they desired. Why would they stay in such a tiny arena when the world was so big? She bit her tongue. Now was not the time to worry over answers to useless questions. Or maybe it was exactly the right time to ask these questions.

Kay smiled. "Many free, arena?"

"Excellent Jangba, Kay. Good job on that accent. And no, not many are free, but a good amount are. It depends on the price of the . . . Am I going too fast for you?"

"No, I learn."

Kindle continued at Kay's nod, and it didn't seem like anyone noticed Kay slip the glass cube map into her pocket.

NINE

RED ROBED BAD GUYS

The lesson dragged on for another hour or so before Kay was finally excused for the evening. Ash had brought Kay her dinner, so she took it to her room where she could eat and study her stolen map in silence.

It truly was beautiful. The glass cube filled her palm and caught the light from the fading sun. The soft glow made the cube gleam and sparkle. She'd completed phase one of the plan. Assuming things went well on Wallace's end, they were now prepared for phase two. Kay figured she would learn about the next phase in the morning, and she wondered just how many phases she would have to complete before she was free.

She turned her attention back to the glass map and set herself the task of memorizing as many of the catacomb pathways as she could.

There was a strange sound in her room. Kay opened her eyes and blinked rapidly, trying to adjust her eyesight to the dark space. She must have fallen asleep while she studied the map. Her boots were still on.

There. The sound again. Light footsteps by her doorway. She squinted in the darkness, catching sight of the figure coming toward her.

Kay screamed.

Her attacker leaped forward and Kay Breathed in, prepared to shoot flames.

"Wallace!" Her flame sputtered out.

"Shh, keep your voice down! Why are you screaming at me?"

"You scared me!" Kay Breathed in again, but this time only to quiet her racing heart.

"I didn't mean to scare you. I thought you were meeting me at midnight." Wallace came closer and sat on one of the empty beds next to her own.

"Sorry, I fell asleep." Now that her eyes were accustomed to the darkness, she could see Wallace's expression. He frowned.

"I guess you'll need another day to complete phase one."

"No, I got it." Kay fumbled around the bed until her fingers grasped the smooth glass cube. She held it up, waving it slightly in the air. "See? I got it right here."

Wallace gave a muted yelp of delight. "I knew you could do it. Did I tell you, or did I tell you? We're getting out of here."

"You got your item too?" Kay handed the glass map over reluctantly. The cube disappeared under Wallace's quick fingers.

He stood up, examining the map in the waning moonlight.

"Oh yeah, take a look." He gestured down to himself with a flourish and Kay frowned.

"What is it?"

"The robes! I'm wearing one of the red robes." He did a quick spin for good measure. The robe was a bit long. The fabric brushed the floor and trailed beyond his fingers. He grinned.

"Where did you get one of those?"

Wallace shrugged. "Stole it. Like you did with this guy." He tossed the glass cube up in the air and caught it, ignoring Kay's startled gasp. "Wasn't easy either. You ever run into one of the red robes?"

Kay nodded, remembering her earlier experience with Kindle.

"Who are they?"

Wallace shrugged. "The guys in charge as far as I can tell. There's all these rules, right? Cadets can't go in the halls, the Fire Dancers can't— "

"And the Red Robes make the rules!" Kay interrupted. She ducked her head and cast a furtive look around once she realized how loud she'd been.

"Yeah, they're the rule makers all right. And they don't seem very nice." He paused. His big brown eyes stared intently at her. "It's probably best you stay away from them. That's something else I wanted to talk to you about. You gotta tone it down."

"Tone what down?"

"Everything. Look, I know you don't speak Jangba, but everyone's talking about the new powerful cadet. *You*. You have to stop showing off. Stop it or you'll ruin everything."

"I haven't done anything." Kay Breathed in and clenched her teeth.

Wallace raised his eyebrows. "Oh yeah? You're not Breathing in right now?"

Kay expelled her breath in a low whoosh, and the heat left her body without producing any flames. She felt oddly deflated.

"Everyone's really talking about me?" she whispered.

"Yeah." Wallace's face softened. "They call you the wonder child. You're really special."

His expression turned serious. "That's why you need to tone it down. You've probably already attracted the attention of the red robes and they're bad news. Trust me."

Kay nodded.

"Good. Do well in training . . . but not too well. Do you understand? We need to keep to ourselves, but not until after phase two is completed." Wallace grinned. The tiny glass cube sent prisms of light onto his face, giving the boy an otherworldly look. "You did good, kid. Now it's time for phase two."

Kay was so excited to hear about phase two, she decided she didn't care that he called her "kid." She scooted closer until she was just barely on the edge of her bed.

"What's phase two? I hope it doesn't involve more stealing."

"Heh, you really like to follow the rules, don't you?" Wallace shrugged and carried on before she could defend herself. "Not to worry, I can do phase two on my own. Now that I have the items from phase one anyway."

"So now we're in phase two?" Kay asked.

"Yup. And it does involve more stealing . . . sort of. We need some food and water. But they would have given it to us anyway, so really I'm just collecting our things. I may need a distraction from you though. Think you can manage that?"

Kay knew that she could.

TEN

PHASE TWO

Kay felt groggy the following morning. Last night almost seemed like some distant dream, but then she noticed the rumpled bed where Wallace had sat. Last night was real. Wallace said it was only a matter of time before they completed their plan. Only a matter of time before she was home. She drank her water and rubbed the sleep out of her eyes before tugging on her stiff boots. Ash was likely waiting for her at the fields, and once again she was late. She only just remembered to grab her practice assegai, snatching the thing as she ran out the door.

Ash was waiting for her on the practice field, but he didn't appear angry. He smiled as he waved her over. Kay let out a small sigh of relief. So he hadn't noticed the stolen map. *Yet.* With any luck, she would be long gone by the time he did. For the first time since Wallace had broached the subject of her return home, Kay felt a small twinge of regret. Ash had been kind to her. She picked up her pace and jogged across the field, panting lightly when she reached Ash's side.

"Today you start training with the other cadets." Ash gestured to the boys behind him. They were assembling into two neat lines. The big guy—Timber was his name—directed the class.

It was weird joining a class led by him. In a small way, she wouldn't be here now if it wasn't for him. She'd only showed her powers to help Kindle. And why had he been sparring so roughly? Shouldn't all the Fire Dancers be friends?

With some hesitation, she took her place beside Wallace in the second line. He pretended not to notice her. He was good at remembering not to draw attention their way. She would get better at it too. Her feet slid into first position.

It was much different training with the other cadets. For one, she was the smallest. She shouldn't have taken her place in the second line. She couldn't see Timber—couldn't see anything except for the tall boys spinning around her. It was hard to hear him too, or maybe she just couldn't understand his instructions. Kay realized just how much she'd come to rely on Kindle's translations. Kay hadn't even bothered learning the correct word in Jangba and instead had given her own names to the range of motions found in each Form. She turned to do a cartwheel kick thingy but realized halfway through she was supposed to be doing a jump forward roll. She frowned. Stupid Jangba. The language sprang from Timber's lips in a quick rolling accent that was impossible to understand. Why couldn't she learn this language faster? Why hadn't her parents taught it to her as Wallace's parents had so clearly taught him? She looked over at him. His movements were clumsy and she wondered if that was because he was just trying to remain in the background or if it was because he truly couldn't do the moves. She sighed. Maybe it didn't matter what Timber was saying. Maybe it was better if she just melted into the background too.

The boy in front of her did a sudden jerking pirouette before dropping down and sweeping out his leg. Yes, from the Red Form. Kay stumbled through the move, frowning when her foot failed to sweep out as the other boy's had.

The deep rolling accent was suddenly in her ear and she jerked to a halt, falling down to the hot sand.

Wallace gave her a glance but did nothing to help her back up to her feet.

When she tried to stand, Timber's large hand came crashing down on her shoulder, pinning her to the ground.

Ash growled something out and Kay recognized the word for "careful," but she was unsure if he was talking to her or to Timber. The man truly was huge, bigger than Ash or Daddy. His big hands looked capable of crushing her without any effort, but she wasn't frightened. She took a deep breath, a normal one, and reminded herself that she wasn't scared. The giant man repeated his words, but they were still a garbled mess of sounds and she shook her head. What was he saying? He didn't bother to slow down his words at all. Was he still mad at her for that wall of fire?

"He says you need to balance your weight on both your back leg and hand equally when you do the floor sweep— " Wallace broke off when Timber began speaking. Whatever he said, Wallace didn't translate, but the tips of his ears reddened and he fell back to practicing the move he had been doing just before. A simple duck and turn.

Kay took a deep Breath before shrugging Timber off her. *I can do this. Equal weight on both sides.* She felt the tip of her tongue slide out in concentration and she bit the end as she turned, smiling when her leg swept out in a straight line behind her. *I did it.*

Timber walked away from her without muttering another

word. She turned toward Wallace, but when she met his eyes, he shook his head with a scowl. Ash's shout was enthusiastic, and she gave him a triumphant grin. At least someone was proud of her.

She decided to "tone it down" for fire motion class. She waited her turn and did exactly as Ash asked, without any extra tricks. It was a solo class, just her and Ash in the arena, and she liked it that way. She'd had enough of Timber's yelling and Wallace's scowling. Today's objective was simple. She had to move a single flame in circles around the unlit torches, lighting them all one by one, then extinguish the flame and do it again. It wasn't hard exactly, but Breathing in and out so frequently in the hot sun left her short of breath. In a good way. It reminded her of the times she'd played with Daddy. They'd had all sorts of games. Hide-and-seek, fetch the flame . . . She smiled in memory.

It would be wonderful to be back home. To feel the gentle breeze on her face—to see grass again.

Ash called her to a halt, and she extinguished the flame abruptly, Breathing it back in. Ash watched with interest.

"Kindle says you call that Breathing. Can you tell me more about that?"

The tanned skin of Ash's face wrinkled in concern. The deep lines spread out from his dark eyes as they squinted against the sun. It was always a cloudless day in the Sand Sea.

Was Ash truly happy here? Could anyone be? He still stared at her expectantly, and Kay realized he waited for some sort of answer. She shook her head. Kay could barely describe it in her own language. There was no way she could stumble through an explanation in Jangba.

Ash nodded as though he understood. "It must be . . . hard. You must feel as though your old life has slipped away, that you can never be happy again." He cut himself off with a snort.

Kay continued to stare up at him, processing his words. He was right. She wouldn't be happy again, not until she was back home on her family's land.

Ash patted her shoulder. "Right then, let's get some conditioning in before dinner."

Kay exhaled her Breath without flame and the world instantly became dimmer. It was time for phase two. Kay threw herself to the ground and began rolling in the hot sand.

"What's happened?" Ash fell to his knees beside her, groaning from the effort.

In response she screamed as loudly as she could and burst into tears. Ash looked horrified.

"Kay!" Ash gripped her shoulder.

"Ow, ow!" Kay let out another loud scream. Timber approached and a few cadets began to crowd around her.

She ignored everyone's questions of what was wrong and continued howling and rolling about in the sand. Everyone crowded around her, their faces twisted in concern. She hoped Wallace had slipped away.

ELEVEN

FAKERS AND SHAKERS

When she was sure Wallace was gone, Kay thrust her foot up in the air and began the noble effort of quieting her tears.

Kindle shoved her way through the crowd and kneeled on Kay's other side.

"What is it? What's happened? Did you twist your ankle? Did something bite you?" The questions toppled over one another as Kindle ran knowing fingers up the length of her legs and spine.

Kay shook her head. "It just hurts."

"What hurts? Tell me so we can help you."

Had Wallace made it? Had she given him enough time? There was no way to be sure.

"Everything!" Kay wailed. "Everything hurts. My feet and— "

Kindle stood up. She snapped a few harsh words in Jangba and the small crowd dispersed.

"Get up, Cadet." Kindle's words were harsh.

Kay stared at her in surprise.

"You heard me," Kindle repeated. "Get. Up."

Kay stood up, slowly. She was unsure if she should still make a show of it, so she hobbled toward Ash, leaning on her assegai for support.

"Cadet"—there was an edge of warning to her voice— "stop pretending to be injured and tell me what is going on."

"My feet hurt and m-my back . . ." Kay trailed off. Kindle didn't look sympathetic. She looked angry. Kay Breathed in.

"Stop lying, Cadet."

"How do you know she is lying?" Ash questioned.

"Trust me, she is."

"But you should have seen her, screaming in the sand. She— "

"She's faking. Are you tired? Trying to end practice early?"

"I don't think she's faking it. We had a good practice today. She did well in fire motion and even Timber was pleased by her display of the Forms."

He continued to ramble on in her defense when Kay realized she'd understood every word he said. She exhaled her Breath in an excited whoosh of smoke, but as she did so, Ash's speech once again became garbled and incoherent.

What was that? Somehow, Kay had understood Jangba perfectly. It was like Ash had been speaking Drakori. But how could that be possible? And if it was, what did it mean? She realized the two adults were staring at her expectantly.

Once again she had lied, only this time, Kindle caught her. So what should she do now? Kay wondered if it was time to admit she was lying. Admit everything. But no, she couldn't do that. She *had* to lie.

"I hurt," she whispered.

Ash looked sad. Kindle took her hand. "All right, Cadet. Let's go for a walk."

Kay allowed herself to be pulled toward the edge of the practice sands. She didn't bother to remain limping.

"They found me at a new year festival when I was nine," Kindle said in Drakori.

Kay thought of the festival last year. The games and the sweet cakes. Daddy always sneaked her a piece before the final hour celebration, even though it made Mama angry.

"I knew what it meant," Kindle continued. "My family, we . . . They're traveling merchants. With a route that runs as far north as La'Nor and then nearly to here, stopping in Scim." Kindle smiled. "Scim, now that's a fun town. In any case, I knew what it was to be marked by the gods. Chosen by the Everflame. And even though I knew the greatness I was marked for, I ran. We both did. It was her idea to run. Once we realized they were coming for us, once we realized we still had that choice. We ran . . . We *tried* to run. She was my twin, you see? She was eight minutes older and she was so bossy. We ran and they caught us. Well, they caught me. Evanee got away and I couldn't follow. And that's how I got this." She pointed to the devilish scar above her eyebrow. "I am . . . content with my life here. But Evanee, she would have never been happy. She was always shaking things up. She challenged people—she challenged me. I miss her every day." Kindle's grip on Kay's hand tightened, and Kay squeezed it back.

Why was Kindle telling her all this? She felt terrible for lying to her. Like there was something rotten in her belly, clawing its way out her throat. Kay swallowed hard.

"You remind me of her. Sometimes she would just be so full of emotion, it would just bubble out of her. Is that what happened, over there? Is that why you got so upset?"

Kay didn't know how to answer. They stood holding hands on the edge of the practice ring for some time.

"I'm sorry," Kay said finally. Because she was sorry. Somehow she had made Kindle feel bad, and she had never wanted that.

"And you're forgiven. But injuries are serious here in the arena and not something to play pretend. You scared me. I don't want to see you hurt."

Kay thought about that. Kindle seemed to mean it. But how could that be true? "But . . . you want me to learn to be a Fire Dancer? You want me to fight?"

Kindle was quiet for so long that Kay didn't think she would answer her, but then she whispered the words as she let go of Kay's hand.

"No, I don't want you to fight."

TWELVE

The Short Farewell

*P**ractice was over. Kindle pulled* Kay close for a hug and Kay squeezed her tightly. She would miss Kindle, but she knew she could never stay here. Kindle had said Kay reminded her of her sister, so maybe she would understand why Kay had to go, why she had to be free.

Ash seemed like he wanted to talk with her some more. He lingered in the doorway of her barracks, and Kay was glad Wallace had taken the glass map with him because Ash's eyes swept across the room, taking in everything.

She hustled to make her bed, though Ash didn't say anything about it. He didn't say anything at all. His silence made Kay uncomfortable.

If everything was going as planned, Wallace would retrieve her in a few hours. They would leave through the catacombs and leave the Sand Sea behind them, forever.

"You are doing well here, Cadet."

Easy words, though praise was rare from Ash, especially outside the arena. She thought again about the weird experience earlier. When she held the flame and understood Ash's words. She Breathed in but felt no different and she stumbled to follow what Ash said next.

"I know this is a difficult time for you, difficult to let go of the life you left behind. But you truly are marked for greatness."

She blinked at him. Had she understood him correctly? She didn't feel great. She only felt alone.

"Get some rest, Cadet. I'll see you in the morning." He carefully leaned her practice assegai against the doorframe. He must have picked it up from where she'd forgotten it in the sands. She hated the thing, but she also felt terrible for leaving it behind. She frowned, trying to work out the tumble of emotions.

Kay nodded her farewell. She told herself that it didn't matter if she didn't hug Ash good-bye. It would only make him suspicious. He shuffled off and she watched him leave.

It seemed she would wait forever. She'd fallen asleep at one point and had jolted from her bed in a panic only to discover the double gong signifying her last chance for dinner. Her belly rumbled a small complaint, and she munched on some leftover flatbread from lunch. Ash never removed her bedside snack, a small wonder for Kay, who had grown up with Mama forbidding any snacks in her room. Kay munched on the bread and continued to wait.

When she thought she might once again fall asleep, she heard a faint scratch at her door. She opened the door wide, too wide, and Wallace stumbled in, tripping over his oversized robe.

"I've got the supplies. Are you ready?"

She was certainly not, but she didn't want Wallace to know. She didn't want him to think that she wasn't brave.

"I was waiting so long." She wasn't trying to complain, not really, but he *had* taken much longer than he had said.

"Yeah, I thought I might run into a little trouble, but I shook it."

He is a shaker too, Kay thought. *Like Kindle's sister. Like me.*

"I'm ready." She tightened the laces on her boots and paused by her assegai, considering. She hated the thing, but Wallace had brought his. It was strapped to his back like how Timber wore his when he wasn't using it. *I won't need it anymore*, she told herself. She left it leaning against the wall and followed Wallace toward her freedom.

It was dark out. And quiet, as the two crept along the edge of the barracks and toward the arena halls. Kay's stomach tumbled wildly and her skin tingled. They were actually leaving. She was going home. No one was outside or in the grand entry halls.

"This is the part that gets tricky," Wallace whispered to her. "We have to make sure no one sees us. I have my disguise, but you . . ." He trailed off and Kay could see his eyes giving her a careful once-over in the moonlight.

"Why didn't you get me a red robe too?" She tried not to let the hurt come across, but she heard it in her tone.

Wallace snorted. "I can barely wear the one I got. There isn't one small enough for a tiny kid like you, and you would look ridiculous."

Kay frowned. Well, he didn't need to be so mean.

"Don't worry kid. I'm getting us out of here. Just stay close. Hopefully it's late enough that everyone will be sleeping. Get ready to move when I say."

She got as close as she could, rolling on the balls of her feet. Her heart beat so hard in her chest, she could hear it hammering in her ears and wondered if Wallace could hear it too. She Breathed in a small amount of heat from the desert around them, still hot despite the disappearance of the sun. Her heartbeat slowed just a bit.

"All right kid, move. Now."

THIRTEEN

THE CATACOMBS

It was hard to stay close to Wallace. He was faster than she was, and when she did manage to get close, she stepped on his robe and caused him to trip. Somehow, they made it into the halls without notice.

They were like Kay remembered—empty save for the torches lining the walls. The memory of her last Breath from these torches pulled at her, but Kay couldn't think about any of that now.

"Keep on the lookout. I need just a second." Wallace had pulled out Ash's glass map. He squinted at it under the torchlight, and Kay resisted the urge to bounce up and down. They didn't have time for this, right? They should be running. Where was the way out? Why hadn't he marked it?

Just when Kay thought she couldn't stand it any longer, Wallace slipped the map back into his pocket and pulled her to the hallway just ahead and to the right.

"Down here," he muttered. "This is the way out."

They hurried down the hall, not quite running when they

arrived at a staircase. Wallace nodded when she sent him a hesitant stare. There was some light ahead, and Kay told herself that even though it was a scary stone stepway leading into the dark underground, she wouldn't be frightened. She couldn't be frightened, not now. Not when she was about to break free.

They saw fewer torches after they descended the stairs. Kay's eyes adjusted fairly easily, then it wasn't so bad as long as she didn't focus on the scary tunnel or the fact that she had done so many bad things to lead her here, or the fact that she still felt torn about her lies to Kindle and her theft from Ash. She didn't mention any of her worries out loud. Wallace was a good friend, and he didn't deserve to feel bad. Not when he was working so hard to get them free. And to think, she had almost messed everything up. What if Kindle had noticed her fake injury and saw it for the distraction it was? In the morning, when they discovered her gone, would Kindle know then that everything Kay had done was all part of a big lie? And what would Ash think when he came to check on her and bring her water in the middle of the night? He would—

"Wallace!"

"What? Keep your voice down," he hissed.

"Ash. My trainer. He brings me water every night. He'll know before morning practice! He— "

"Shh. Okay. I got it. We just have to hurry, that's all. We're almost there I think." He fumbled with the map, trying to read it, but they weren't under a torch, and the detailed etching was hard to make out in the darkness. "Just keep going." Wallace muttered, shoving his hand and the map back down into his pocket. He must have misjudged the distance or maybe it was because the robe was just too big, but the glass map missed the pocket and fell to the floor, shattering into hundreds of tiny pieces.

Kay couldn't keep the loud gasp from escaping her lips. The map! Now what would they do? She was about to ask him when she noticed a dancing flame behind him. It bobbed up and down, and it seemed to be coming closer. They were being followed.

"Wallace." Kay grabbed at his arm.

"Run!" he shouted. Because it didn't matter how loud he was. They were caught and quickly losing their only chance at an escape.

Kay hurried after him, stumbling over her own feet and swinging her arms wildly for balance. She Breathed in out of habit, and an idea struck as she did. She Breathed in the flame from their pursuer's torch. There, let them chase her in the dark.

Wallace was much quicker than she was, but somehow she managed to keep up.

"Stop! Stop. Who's down here?" The voice, booming and deeply authoritative, reverberated down the stone hallway.

Not Ash then. Perhaps they were only being chased because they were down where they didn't belong? For some reason, the fact that they were being pursued by someone aside from Kindle or Ash made Kay feel better.

"This way, kid." Wallace's voice called out to her from the right and she turned sharply, running faster to keep up. What did it matter who was chasing them? She had to escape.

She pumped her arms as fast as they would go, but she worried it wasn't fast enough. She could hear the steady slap of multiple feet hitting stone. It sounded like there was more than one person chasing them.

"Hurry, Kay. Keep up," Wallace growled from up ahead. "Turn left!" he shouted.

She turned blindly, catching a glimpse of his silhouette before he made another sharp turn. She could just make out his form up ahead. She ran to it, surprised by how easily she caught up—surprised to see he wasn't moving but panting hard. Had he waited for her to catch up? She was about to yell at him to keep going when she realized why he'd stopped. There was nowhere else to run. They were at the smooth stone wall of a dead end.

FOURTEEN

SOMETHING SPECIAL

K ay shook her head. *As if she could shake the truth away.*
As if she could shake herself awake and find the last
few weeks had all been some terrible dream. It was
over. They could never escape now. Not now, when they literally
had no place left to run.

Wallace removed the hooded robe, allowing it to pool on
the floor at his feet. He pulled at the assegai strapped to his back
and Kay choked back a gasp. Surely he didn't mean to fight
whoever chased them, did he? But he placed his weapon on the
floor before stepping over it and pressing his palms into the stone
wall.

Wallace Breathed. At least, it seemed that way. Kay could
feel the pull of heat toward him, the static energy that sizzled
alive inside him. She knew the sensation but had only previously
felt it next to Daddy when he Breathed. But Wallace didn't
produce any flame. He didn't seem to do anything at all. But Kay
had felt his intake of Breath and its release. Felt him once again
Breathe beside her.

"Help me," he gasped. He pushed into the wall as though he could push the wall open.

"I don't understand." Kay struggled to keep from whining. They were running out of time. The racing footsteps were deafening in the stone hall. Kay could make out the distant shadows running toward them in the darkness beyond.

"Come on, kid. You're stronger than I am. Help me. I can't melt this alone."

Kay felt him Breathe again so she did too, though she was unsure what to do next. Wallace continued to push into the wall, he pushed the *heat* into the wall. Understanding dawned on her. He was Breathing, but instead of expelling the heat as flames, he let it go into the wall. He wanted to melt the stone and make their own way out of there. Kay pressed her palms beneath him into the stone. The wall was scalding hot, but Kay didn't mind — she never minded the heat.

She had never used her power in this way before. The wall seemed capable of sucking in an endless supply of heat. It felt strange to Breathe in so much without the satisfaction of expelling flames. But different didn't make it wrong. She Breathed in more, focusing hard even though a tiny hole had begun to form in the stone. More — they needed more. Kay Breathed in all she could, reaching out for the distant torches and sucking in their flames. The hole widened, clumps of molten rock falling away. Yes, they were doing it! Kay wanted to demand answers from Wallace. She wanted to know if he could make his own flame too. Or if he just knew this trick here, of melting the stone. He was special too, and once they were free, there would be more that he could show her and perhaps that she could show him. She wouldn't be alone. She pushed everything she had into the boiling stone, felt it crumple and squish between her fingers. This was it; they were free.

"Stop that, right now. This instant. What do you two think you are doing?"

Kay ignored the voice. It seemed to come from right behind her, but she didn't care. They were almost done. The hole was big enough for her to squeeze through and with just a bit more, Wallace too. Rough hands grabbed her arm, pulling her backward. "You're not going anywhere."

FIFTEEN

GREAT BALLS OF FIRE

O*n instinct, Kay Breathed. The* man holding her released his grip on her arm with a yelp. Kay drew out a ball of fire, holding it in front of her. There were three of them. Red robes, although Kay didn't recognize any as the ones she'd encountered before. Maybe they didn't know who she was.

"Easy there, cadets. You haven't done anything that can get you into too much trouble—yet."

The man was short despite the fact that his voice was deep and loud. He fixed Kay with a careful stare. "Release the flame, Cadet, and I'll see that Ash gets his wonder child back unharmed."

"She doesn't speak Jangba," Wallace said at her side. But she *had* understood, Kay realized. It was happening again. She released the flame by Breathing it back in. She would stay ready.

The short man exchanged looks with his robed companions.

"I think she understands well enough. Isn't that right, Cadet?" Kay met his stare and narrowed her eyes.

"You cadets are lucky we found you when we did. Trying

to burn your way right out of the arena, were you? I've never seen anything like it. I see why you are called his wonder child. Never mind if you had kept at it you would have been lucky if you had kept the walls and ceiling from crumbling in on you. You have to know you just can't start breaking down walls in an underground structure . . ." He trailed off. His eyes hardened again before he pointed a wagging finger at Kay. "Now, I will escort you cadets back to your barracks, and in the morning we can discuss proper punishment."

"We're not going back." Wallace slowly bent to the ground and retrieved his assegai. His feet slid into first position.

No. He couldn't fight them, even if he had toned his true skill down, even if he was the greatest fighter ever—as good as Timber or her daddy. He wouldn't be able to take on three people. Not all at one time. They were trapped. It was over before it had even begun. Maybe that was the problem. Maybe Kay had been silly to think she could ever escape. No, she was the wonder child of the arena, and she was never going home. She took a careful step toward the red robes.

But Wallace was like her. He didn't belong here. He needed to be free.

She turned around. The stone wall held a gaping hole. She could dart through it now, make a run for it. An impossible breeze stirred from outside. One simple leap through and she would have her freedom.

But for how long? They would keep chasing her well after she left the arena. Maybe all the way back to her home. They could still get her and bring her back. They had done so before. She had been so close to freedom, and yet in a way, she had never been close at all.

They would never stop pursuing her. She could never be free. But Wallace could. He deserved it. And this was the only way. She still held so much Breath. She smiled at Wallace.

"Thank you for being my friend," she said in Drakori before she kicked him in the chest as hard as she could. He stumbled back toward the hole, toward his freedom. She Breathed in just a bit more then pushed all the fire she could into one spot. One giant flame after another rolled over her in a spectacular explosion of heat and color. For one long moment, nothing happened, then the walls came tumbling down.

Her head hurt. A lot. Kay struggled to open her eyes, blinking against the harsh morning sun. Ash stood at her bedside. He beamed at her, the smile reminding her of her daddy. She was instantly saddened by the memory and turned away to find Kindle seated on the bed beside her.

Kindle reached for Kay's hand and gave it a small squeeze. "You had us worried there."

Kay blinked. This was a lot to take in first thing in the morning. Was this because of what she'd done yesterday? The big ball of flames she'd produced to stop Timber had probably been a bad thing, but Ash and Kindle hadn't seemed too upset about it last night, had they? The events from the night before were fuzzy and Kay wasn't quite sure why.

She sat up, but that sent the room twirling and she brought her hand up to her head, surprised to find it wrapped in gauzy material. She rubbed at the material until a tender spot near her hairline made her pull her hand back with a whimper.

"What happened to my head?" she asked Kindle. Her throat was scratchy and her hands smelled like smoke.

"You whacked it pretty fierce during last night's adventure."

"I did?" Kay frowned, trying to remember. She was tired and seemed only to remember being sleepy but no, she had made that wall of fire and that was probably a bad thing.

"And a sore head is only the beginning of the repercussions from last night," a sharp voice said. Kay turned to see a short man wagging his finger at her. There was something familiar in the gesture, but Kay couldn't recall seeing the man before. He wore a long, hooded red robe. The robe reminded her of something too, but she couldn't remember what. Trying to remember only made her head hurt worse so she squeezed her eyes tight.

"I'm sorry, Kindle," she murmured. "I won't throw fire at the bad man anymore."

Kindle frowned. "It's all right, Cadet."

Kay wrinkled her nose. How had Kindle forgotten her name already? She held back a tired yawn and fixed another stare at the short man in red. He seemed ready to boil over in anger.

"No, it is not all right. You three can't comprehend the damage I have to repair after last night. And someone will be held accountable." Kindle repeated the words in Drakori after Kay asked her what the man was upset about.

"I . . . made a mess last night? And that's how I hurt my head?" Kay frowned. It was a struggle to follow everything.

"A mess?" The man in red snorted. "The damage to the catacombs alone will take months to repair, never mind the amount the council will have to pay to keep this quiet from the Thirteen and the— "

"That's enough," Ash grumbled. "We get the point."

"Kay." Kindle's voice was worried, and her grip on Kay tightened. At least she remembered her name again. "What's the last thing you remember?"

The simple question held such a serious edge that Kay trembled as she gave her answer. "We talked in sand."

Kindle nodded encouragingly. "Yes, in the practice sands. You and I talked and then?"

Kay shook her head. Perhaps this was the explanation behind the feeling of dread within her. She was suddenly overcome with the inexplicable desire to tell the truth, to admit everything. "I talked to the fat man in Drakori and . . . I lied." Her voice fell to a whisper. "I lied to everyone and said that I didn't know what it meant to move fire but really I did." She swallowed as the realization sank in. "I'm being punished because I lied and made fire when I wasn't supposed to."

Kindle looked stunned. Ash sat down heavily on the bed, causing it to groan under the sudden weight. He pulled a hand down the length of his face.

"Is that truly the last thing you remember? Making a big fire so I could escape from Timber?" Kindle sounded sad and Kay swallowed. She had done something else to make Kindle sad, but she didn't understand just what.

Kindle nodded. "I think this cadet has had enough questioning about the incident."

She repeated the words and an endless stream of others to the two men in the room, and moments later everyone shuffled out.

Kindle paused in the doorway, pointing to a long stick leaning against the wall. "You'll begin your training again in the morning. See that you bring your assegai and . . . see that you get some rest between now and then." She offered Kay another sad smile.

Something about that word tugged at Kay's memory, but she was tired and her head was still spinning. Why did Kindle keep referring to her as cadet, and who was that man in red? She hadn't meant to make everyone angry. She just wanted to get back home.

"Kindle? Am I in trouble?" She had to ask. Punishment didn't seem fair. Not when she hadn't done anything but defend her friend, not when she already had this pounding headache.

"No," Kindle answered, "you're not in trouble." She closed the door softly behind her and Kay stared at the new wooden pole leaning against the wall. Kindle had said something about training in the morning. Did that mean she got to learn how to dance with the long stick like she had seen the boys doing? That had looked like fun. Besides, she had to fit in until she could figure out a way to escape. Until she could find her way back home.

ACKNOWLEDGMENTS

This novelette would not be possible without some wonderful people I'm lucky enough to call mine. Biggest of all thanks to my father, Rick Marrero. Without the hours of long conversation and your random ideas, this little story may never have been completed! Author Melody Greene, thanks for your endless support and for just being present anytime I needed someone to talk me off my crazy or to give me the encouragement to continue. I can't thank Kingsman Editing enough. This wonderful team has taken my story and truly made it shine! Cayce Berryman deserves an award for all my endless Facebook messages and her sage advice. Huge thanks to all of my readers for placing faith in a new author. I hope you enjoy *Fetch the Flame*!

ABOUT THE AUTHOR

Alexis Marrero Deese is an avid reader of Young Adult and fantasy. Her favorite authors include Brandon Sanderson and Jaqueline Carey. She graduated from the University of South Florida with a Bachelor's Degree in Creative Writing. *Ignited*, book one of the Dance of the Elements series, is her debut novel. When she isn't writing, Alexis is probably cooking an elaborate meal, enjoying the outdoors with her three dogs or wasting her day on Pinterest.

FETCH THE FLAME

KAY'S INTERLUDE

Learn more about A.M. Deese
and explore her other titles at
www.amdeese.com